SCOOBY-DOO!

and the

SUNKEN SHIP

Written by James Gelsey
Illustrations by Duendes del Sur

WORLDWIDE PUBLISHING

Curious Fox

For Jason

First published in this format in 2014 by Curious Fox,
an imprint of Capstone Global Library Limited,
7 Pilgrim Street, London, EC4V 6LB
– Registered company number: 6695582

www.curious-fox.com

CAPG33550

Originated by Capstone Global Library Ltd
Printed and bound in Spain by Grafos S.A.

ISBN 978 1 782 02152 0
18 17 16 15 14
10 9 8 7 6 5 4 3 2 1

A CIP catalogue record for this book is available
from the British Library.

Chapter 1

"Turn here, Fred," Daphne said suddenly.

Fred made a sharp right turn. The Mystery Machine went slowly down a narrow, curving road. "Are you sure this is the way to Sandy Cove, Daphne?" Fred asked.

"I'm positive," Daphne replied. She pointed to a large oak tree up ahead. "I remember that big tree from when my family used to come here. Aunt Maggie says that is the oldest tree in Sandy Cove. I can't wait to see her and Uncle Murray."

"According to this guidebook," Velma said,

"Sandy Cove is one of the oldest towns in the whole area."

"Oh, yes," Daphne said. "I'm so happy that we're going to spend the weekend. Sandy Cove has the prettiest town square and the best beaches, too."

"And the best excuse to eat french fries I've ever heard of," Shaggy added.

Velma turned around to the back seat where Shaggy was sitting. "What are you talking about?" she asked.

"Like, that sign we just passed," Shaggy explained. "It said 'Welcome to Fry Fest.' Imagine, a whole town devoted to french fries."

"Rummy," Scooby-Doo barked, rubbing his belly.

"Shaggy, it's Frye Fest," Daphne said. "Spelled F-r-y-e."

"As in french fry," Shaggy said eagerly.

"As in Captain Horace P. Frye," Velma said, correcting him. "He's a pirate who lived in Sandy Cove over three hundred years ago. That's where they got the name Frye Fest."

"No rench ries?" Scooby asked.

"I'm sure there will be french fries, Scooby," Daphne reassured him.

"Pirate, huh?" Shaggy said. "Then maybe there's some buried treasure."

"I'm not so sure about treasure, Shaggy," Fred said. "But I have heard there's going to be some terrific fireworks."

"The town's just up ahead," Daphne said. "I can't wait to see Sandy Cove again. I can still picture all the friendly people and beautiful little shops on the High Street."

The van drove under a big white arch and into town. Daphne couldn't believe her eyes. Most of the buildings looked run-down. Some were even boarded up. Except for a handful of people, the streets were empty.

There was nothing beautiful about this town.

"Are you sure this is Sandy Cove?" Fred asked.

"Yes," Daphne said sadly. "But everything looks so different."

The Mystery Machine continued down the High Street. At the end of the street was a huge

statue of a man holding a sword above his head.
He had one foot resting on a treasure chest.

"Maybe he's scaring everyone away,"
Shaggy said. "I'd hate to bump into him in the
dark."

"You don't have to worry about meeting him, Shaggy," Velma said. "That's the famous Captain Frye. He's been dead for over three hundred years."

"Even more reason not to bump into him," Shaggy said.

"Rou said it!" Scooby agreed.

Fred steered the Mystery Machine into the driveway of the Sandy Cove Hotel.

"Don't let the way things look get you down, Daphne," Fred said. "We're still going to have a great time."

"I hope you're right," Daphne said. "But I'm getting a strange feeling about this place."

Chapter 2

The Sandy Cove Hotel was a large sea green house. It was three storeys tall and had a lot of windows. The gang walked up to the front door and found a note taped there.

"'Please come in around back,'" Daphne read. Daphne turned to the gang. "Follow me."

The gang then followed Daphne along a path that led to the back of the house.

"Jinkies," Velma said when she saw the large beach behind the hotel. "You can see almost all of Brannigan Bay from here."

"And even a little more sometimes," said a strange voice. The gang turned and saw a man wearing a white suit with a white shirt and tie. His trouser legs were rolled up, and he wasn't wearing any shoes.

"If you look over there, past Lucky Grove," the man continued, "you can even see Shining Palms." He pointed towards two palm trees that curved together in the shape of a horseshoe. Looking through the trees, the gang could make out some buildings in the distance.

"That's Shining Palms," the man said. "It's a beautiful resort. Much nicer than anything you'll find here. Take a look." He handed Fred, Daphne,

Velma, and Shaggy slick brochures. They were full of pictures of people swimming, playing in the sand, sailing, and eating.

"Barney Silo!" yelled a woman from the hotel's deck. She walked down the steps to the beach. "You get out of here before I call the sheriff. I've had about enough of you trying to steal our guests away."

Barney Silo smiled and started backing away. "Not even Frye Fest can save this town. It's time you accepted that fact and sold me your land."

The woman was getting angry. "We'll never sell you so much as a glass of lemonade," she said to him. "Now shoo!"

Barney Silo put on a pair of headphones, turned on his portable radio, and walked towards the water. He got into a small rowing boat.

Daphne walked up to the woman and gave her a kiss.

"Hi, Aunt Maggie," she said. "It's so good to see you."

"It's wonderful to see you, too, Daphne," Aunt Maggie replied. "My, how you've grown."

"Did I mention the all-you-can-eat

barbecue tonight?" Barney Silo called as he rowed away.

Shaggy's and Scooby's eyes lit up.

"Did he say all you can eat?" Shaggy asked.

"Forget it, you two," Daphne said. "We're staying here in Sandy Cove."

Scooby put his head down low and Shaggy frowned.

"Don't you worry," Aunt Maggie said. "Tonight's Frye Fest, and it's going to be great."

"Where's Uncle Murray?" Daphne asked.

"He's down by the dock getting things set up for tonight," Aunt Maggie answered. "He'll be back soon. Now then, I've got some fresh lemonade and home-made biscuits up on the deck

for you and your friends."

Aunt Maggie smiled and nodded as Daphne introduced her friends. Scooby-Doo wagged his tail especially fast when she said how smart and brave he looked. "I'm very pleased to meet all of you," Aunt Maggie said. "I hope you'll make yourselves at home here."

"Great!" Shaggy said. "So, like, where's the kitchen?"

"Shaggy," Velma said, giving him a look. "That's not what she means."

"Sorry," Shaggy said.

"Excuse me, Aunt Maggie," Fred said. "But who was that man who was talking to us before?"

Aunt Maggie sat down on one of the deckchairs. "That was Barney Silo," she said. "He owns Shining Palms, the big resort down the beach."

"But what is he doing here?" Velma asked.

Aunt Maggie poured herself a glass of lemonade and sat back. "Barney Silo's buying up as much property on Brannigan Bay as he can. He wants to expand his resort," she said. "Most of the other places along the bay have gone out of business. Sandy Cove is the only town left."

"Is that why you're holding Frye Fest?" Velma asked.

"Yes. Captain Frye is a Sandy Cove legend," Aunt Maggie said. "The Frye Fest is celebrating Captain Frye's three-hundred-and fiftieth birthday. We're hoping the celebration attracts lots of people. Barney Silo's right. If Frye Fest flops, the people of Sandy Cove will have to sell their land to him."

Daphne sat down next to Aunt Maggie. "Is there anything we can do to help make Frye Fest a success?" she asked.

"Just have fun and eat!" Aunt Maggie exclaimed.

"Rou rot it!" Scooby barked.

Chapter 3

After they got settled into their rooms, the gang met back on the deck. Everyone was dressed for the beach.

"Okay, everyone," Fred said, "ready to hit the beach?" Fred looked at Shaggy and Scooby. Shaggy was carrying a bucket and spade. Scooby-Doo was next to him, wearing sunglasses and a purple towel around his neck.

"I can't believe how empty it is," Daphne said as the gang walked down the beach. "When I was a little girl, we could barely find room to walk because there were so many people here."

"Well, I say good riddance!" said a

woman walking by. She was wearing a faded Sandy Cove sweatshirt, an old baseball cap, and headphones connected to a metal detector. As she walked, she swept the metal detector over the sand. She passed Scooby-Doo and the gang and headed over to a young man sitting on the sand. The man was playing with a radio-controlled dune buggy.

"That woman looks familiar to me," Daphne said. She walked over to the woman. "Aren't you Edna Crupzak?" Daphne asked.

The old woman was surprised that Daphne knew her name. "Do I know you?" she asked.

Daphne smiled. "You used to run the ice-cream stand on the beach," she said.

"I didn't think anyone remembered," Edna Crupzak said. "We've been closed ever since Shining Palms opened. All the tourists left us high and dry."

"That's too bad," Velma said.

"Now they're living it up at Shining Palms," Edna said. "And we're left having a birthday party for a dead pirate. I'll tell you, the only good thing that pirate ever did for this town was stay the night."

"And leave his treasure buried somewhere," the young man on the sand said.

"Hush now, Junior," Edna said. "It's time to go."

"Yes, Mummy," the young man answered.

Junior Crupzak gathered his belongings up and started walking down the beach.

Edna turned back to the gang.

"Keep an eye on that Silo fellow," she said. "If you're not careful, he'll try to buy you out, too. He's here every day, handing out brochures. Between you and me, I wish everyone would just leave us alone. At least I'd get some peace and quiet."

Edna turned on her metal detector, put on

her headphones, and walked after Junior.

Velma carefully watched Edna walk away. "If I'm not mistaken," Velma said, "those are Shining Palms brochures in her back pocket."

"That's odd," Daphne said. "I wonder why she'd have all those brochures?"

"Who knows! Listen, gang," Fred said. "We're here to relax, so let's forget about Edna Crupzak and have a good time."

"Fred's right. I'm going to look for seashells," Velma said. "Anyone want to come?"

"Sure," Daphne and Fred said together.

"What are you two going to do?" Daphne asked Shaggy and Scooby.

"Scooby and I are going to build sand castles," Shaggy said, holding up his bucket and spade. "And maybe dig for buried treasure."

"Just don't dig up any trouble," Daphne said.

"Trouble?" Shaggy said. "We're on a beach in a quiet little resort town. Like, what kind of trouble could we get into here?"

"That's just what we don't want to find out," Fred said.

Chapter 4

When Fred, Daphne, and Velma were down the beach, Shaggy turned to Scooby-Doo.

"Hey, Scooby," Shaggy said, reaching into his pocket. "Look what I found in my room." He took out a piece of paper and carefully unfolded it. Scooby-Doo looked closely at the yellowed paper.

"Reasure map!" barked Scooby.

"Shhhhhhhhhh!" Shaggy said, putting his hand over Scooby's mouth. "Like, not so loud, man." Shaggy looked around and then whispered

19

to Scooby, "This is one of Captain Frye's treasure maps. And it says that one of his treasure chests is buried somewhere on this beach. All we have to do is follow the map and dig up the treasure."

"Rench ries for rife!" Scooby said happily.

"That's right, buddy, so let's go," Shaggy said. While Shaggy looked at the map, Scooby sniffed along the sand. He got too close and sniffed some sand into his nose.

"Rah-chooo!" Scooby sneezed.

"Scooby, quit clowning around," Shaggy said. "I'm trying to work out what this picture of a horseshoe means. Like, where are we going to find a horseshoe on the beach?"

Scooby thought a minute and then had an idea. He stood up straight and raised his right paw over his head. Then he raised his left paw over his head. His paws met right over his head, making a horseshoe shape.

"Like, this is no time for exercises, Scooby-Doo," Shaggy said. "We need a horseshoe or else we'll never find the treasure."

"Rucky Grove!" Scooby barked. He acted out again how the two trees leaned towards each other to form the shape of a horseshoe.

"I got it, Scooby-Doo," Shaggy called. "It's the horseshoe-shaped trees that Barney Silo pointed out. I knew I'd work it out. Let's go!"

They ran over to the horseshoe-shaped trees and stood beneath them. Shaggy checked the map again.

"It says here to count off thirty-three paces," Shaggy said. "And we have to walk this way." Shaggy pointed towards the bay.

Shaggy and Scooby stood side by side under the horseshoe trees.

"I'll walk and you count, Scooby," Shaggy said.

Shaggy started walking, taking careful, even steps along the beach.

"Run, roo, ree, rour, rive, rix, reven, reight ..." Scooby counted off.

"Hey, slow down there, Scoob," Shaggy said. "Captain Frye only had two legs like me, not four

like you. Count with my steps."

"Rorry," Scooby apologized. Shaggy started walking again and Scooby continued the count.

"Rine, ren, releven, relve …" At twenty-one, they reached the water's edge.

"Now what do we do?" Shaggy asked.

Before Scooby could answer, they heard a rumbling sound come from the water. Straight ahead out on the bay they saw a huge ship. It had two large masts with huge white sails. On top of the tallest mast was a black-and-white flag waving in the wind.

"That's a pirate flag," Shaggy said. "It

must be a pirate ship." Suddenly, the ship started sinking.

"Zoinks! Look at that," Shaggy exclaimed. "The ship is sinking like a rock." Within moments, the ship disappeared into the water.

"Boy, that was something," Shaggy said. "Wait till the others hear about this."

Shaggy and Scooby turned and started walking back up the beach when they heard another strange sound. They turned and saw an explosion of bubbles burst through the water. Something started walking out of the water. It was covered with seaweed.

With each step, the seaweed creature grabbed clumps of seaweed from its body and threw them down. Bit by bit, the creature was looking more like a man. He was wearing a large blue coat, tall black boots, and a sword around his waist. The man was hunched over a bit and had a patch over his right eye. This was no ordinary man. He was a pirate! He limped forward and took his sword from his waist. The pirate raised it high over his head.

"Arrr, it's good to be back home in Sandy Cove," he said with a scratchy voice.

"Zoinks!" Shaggy gasped. "It's the ghost of Captain Frye! Run, Scooby-Doo, run!"

Chapter 5

Fred, Daphne, and Velma were arriving back at the Sandy Cove Hotel just as Shaggy and Scooby came running up to the deck.

"He's here! We saw him!" Shaggy exclaimed.

"Saw who?" Fred asked.

Scooby stood up on his hind legs. He hunched over, closed one eye, and limped around in a circle.

"Arrrrr," Scooby growled.

"Captain Frye!" Shaggy said. "We saw his pirate ship sink in the bay. Then he emerged from the water and walked onto the beach."

"We saw a ship sink, too," Daphne said. "But we didn't see any pirate."

"Shaggy, that pirate ship is a special effect for Frye Fest tonight," Velma said. "It's supposed to re-enact the sinking of Captain Frye's real ship over three hundred years ago."

Aunt Maggie nodded in agreement. "There will be fireworks, too. That's what Daphne's uncle Murray was working on all morning," Aunt Maggie said. "He'll be pleased that it looked so real."

"Well, if that ship wasn't real, what about that pirate?" Shaggy asked.

"I don't think a pirate's part of the show," Aunt Maggie said. "But maybe they added it at the last minute."

"Or maybe it really is the ghost of Captain Frye," Shaggy said. "And he's mad because he wasn't invited to his own birthday party."

"Arrr, what do we have here, mates?" said a man from the top of the stairs.

"Rikes!" Scooby barked as he dove under Daphne's deckchair.

"Uncle Murray!" Daphne exclaimed. She ran over and gave him a hug.

"Hello, Daphne," Uncle Murray said with a big smile.

Aunt Maggie walked over to her husband. "Your ship was a huge success with Daphne's friends," she said.

"What do you mean?" Uncle Murray asked.

"You know, Uncle Murray," Daphne said.

"The way you made it sink into the bay. It really fooled Shaggy and Scooby."

Shaggy smiled and waved at Uncle Murray. Scooby poked his head out from under the chair.

"Rello," Scooby said.

"I don't see how that can be," Uncle Murray said. "The boat is radio-controlled, and Salty Joe and I spent all morning trying to get it to work. We worked out there was something wrong with the controls. We just gave up on it a little while ago."

The gang all looked at one another.

"You mean you didn't make the boat sink?" Fred asked.

"I'm sorry to say it, but no," Uncle Murray replied.

"Jinkies," Velma said. "Maybe that really was a ghost ship."

Just then, the music stopped coming from the radio. A loud blast of static blared from the speakers. Then a strange voice started speaking.

"Arrrr, attention, Sandy Cove," the voice said. "This is Captain Horace Frye. I warn all of you to leave this place before sundown. I will not warn you again!"

A loud blast of static followed his voice, and then the music began again.

"Zoinks!" Shaggy exclaimed. "Like, that sounded like the pirate Scooby and I saw on the beach. Captain Frye really is here. Make room for me, Scooby!" Shaggy dove under Daphne's deckchair next to Scooby.

Aunt Maggie and Uncle Murray shook their heads. "It looks like somebody doesn't want us to have Frye Fest," Uncle Murray said.

"This is just terrible," Aunt Maggie said.

Daphne put her arm around her aunt. "Don't give up hope yet, Aunt Maggie," she said.

"That's right," Fred added. "Mystery, Inc. is officially on the case. Right, gang?"

"Right!" cheered Shaggy, Daphne, and Velma.

"Right!" barked Scooby from under the chair.

Chapter 6

The gang huddled together on the Sandy Cove Hotel's deck.

"Okay, everybody, we've got a lot of ground to cover if we're going to get to the bottom of this before Frye Fest begins," Fred said. "First and foremost, someone needs to have a look at that mysterious sunken ship."

Fred, Daphne, and Velma all looked at Shaggy and Scooby.

"Not us," Shaggy said. He and Scooby shook their heads.

"You two are the only ones who have seen the pirate," Velma added.

"Plus, you might even find some buried treasure," Daphne said. Shaggy stopped shaking his head and thought for a minute.

"Hmmm, maybe you're right," Shaggy said.

"Ruh-uh," Scooby said.

"Scooby, even if that pirate is there, he's over three hundred years old," Shaggy said. "He'd never be able to outdoggy-paddle you."

"Would you do it for a Scooby Snack?" Daphne asked.

"Rope," Scooby barked.

"How about two Scooby Snacks?" Fred asked.

Scooby just shook his head.

"All right, three Scooby Snacks," Velma said.

"And ruried reasure," Scooby added.

"And buried treasure," Velma agreed.

"Rokay!" Scooby barked.

Velma took three Scooby Snacks from her

beach bag and tossed them into the air, one at a time. Scooby jumped up and gobbled each one down.

"While you go looking for clues," Aunt Maggie said, "we're going to get as many people as we can to stay for Frye Fest tonight."

"Great idea, Aunt Maggie," Daphne said.

"I want to go to the town hall to look up something," Velma said.

"Great," Fred said. "Daphne and I will walk with Shaggy and Scooby to the dock and then look around the beach."

"Shaggy and Scooby should see Salty Joe about diving in the bay," Uncle Murray said. "He's down on the dock right now. He'd be happy to help. Just tell him I sent you."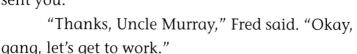

"Thanks, Uncle Murray," Fred said. "Okay, gang, let's get to work."

Velma followed the path around to the front of the house to walk into town. Fred, Daphne,

Shaggy, and Scooby walked to the dock down on the beach.

The dock wasn't anything fancy. It was just a long row of wooden planks that stuck out into the bay. Some of the planks were cracked and a few were even missing. At the end of the dock stood an old wooden shack.

"Good luck, you two," Daphne said. She and Fred continued along the beach.

"I guess this is the place," Shaggy said. "Ready, Scoob?"

"Ruh-uh," Scooby said.

"Me neither," Shaggy said. "You go first." Shaggy gave Scooby a slight push onto the dock.

Scooby started walking carefully along the planks. Shaggy slowly followed. When they got to the end of the dock, Shaggy knocked lightly on the wooden shack's door.

"Hello?" Shaggy called. "Anyone home?"

The door opened and out stepped an old man. He had stubby grey whiskers all over his chin and wore an eye patch.

"A rirate!" Scooby barked as he jumped into Shaggy's arms.

"I'm no pirate," the man said. "Just Salty Joe. What can I do for you?"

"Can you, like, help us with some diving?" Shaggy asked.

"Who sent you?" Salty Joe asked.

"Uncle Murray," Shaggy replied.

"Murray? Why didn't you say so?" Salty Joe said. "I'll be right back."

Salty Joe went back into the shack and came out carrying some diving gear, including fins and face masks.

"Here you go," Salty Joe said. "First-rate scuba diving gear."

"Hey, Scooby, this gear was made just for you," Shaggy said.

"Ruh?" Scooby said.

"Yeah, it's, like, Scooby diving gear," Shaggy joked. "Get it? Scooby? Scuba?" Shaggy and Scooby laughed as Salty Joe helped them put on the gear.

"You breathe through here," Salty Joe explained. "And you'll need this." He handed Shaggy a torch.

"Okay, Scooby," Shaggy said. "Let's go find us some buried treasure."

Chapter 7

Shaggy and Scooby slowly floated down to the bottom of Brannigan Bay. Their feet touched the bottom and Shaggy turned to Scooby to say something.

"Glub glub glub glub glub glub glub," is all that Scooby heard. It was hard to talk underwater wearing scuba gear. Shaggy then pointed in the direction they were supposed to go. The two of them walked along the bottom of the bay. Many kinds of fish swam by. It was hard to keep track of them all. There were red fish and white fish and striped fish and long fish and skinny fish and fat fish.

They swam by a big rock. Shaggy reached over to touch it and it moved! The rock opened its eyes and saw Shaggy and Scooby. It wasn't a rock after all. It was an octopus! It raised its eight arms and waved them at the boys.

"Zoiglub!" Shaggy exclaimed. "Let'sglub goglub!" He and Scooby jumped off the bay floor and started swimming away. They had only gone a few feet when they saw something else in front of them.

As they got closer, they saw it was the sunken ship. Shaggy and Scooby could see parts of the upper deck. Shaggy looked at Scooby and gave him the thumbs-up sign. The buried treasure had to be there.

Shaggy and Scooby swam for a closer look when an explosion of bubbles burst from inside the ship. Captain Frye floated out from the ship. He had his sword in one hand and a torch in the other.

"Arrrr, I warned you to leave Sandy Cove," he said to them. His voice wasn't full of air bubbles

like Shaggy's. "Now you must pay!" Captain Frye
started swimming right at Shaggy and Scooby.

"Rikes, glubs!" Scooby barked. He turned
and doggy-paddled away as fast as he could.

Captain Frye was getting closer. Just as he
was about to grab Scooby's tail, something pulled
Captain Frye back. It was the octopus! Shaggy and
Scooby swam to safety while Captain Frye fought
with the eight-armed creature.

Shaggy and Scooby swam to the dock. Salty Joe helped them up and took off their gear.

"Any luck?" asked Salty Joe.

"Like, only in not getting eaten by an octopus or attacked by Captain Frye," Shaggy said. "Wait till the others hear about this." He and Scooby ran down the dock and straight back to the Sandy Cove Hotel.

Fred, Daphne, and Velma were already waiting on the deck with Aunt Maggie and Uncle Murray.

"We saw Captain Frye again!" Shaggy said. "He was in his ship and he saw us and he chased us with his sword!"

"What was Captain Frye doing when you found him?" Velma asked.

"I think he was looking for something around the sunken ship," Shaggy said. "But when he saw us he stopped and yelled at us. Something about how he warned us to leave Sandy Cove."

"That's odd," Velma said. "People can't speak underwater."

"What did you and Fred find, Daphne?" Uncle Murray asked.

"We found an old rowing boat down the

beach," Daphne said.

"And look what we found inside," Fred added. He showed everyone a handful of wet Shining Palms brochures and a pair of headphones.

"Based on what I learned in town," Velma said, "I have a hunch that this pirate ghost wants more than just a quiet holiday in his old home."

"I think Velma's right," Fred added. "It's time to set a trap to catch this ghost. And there's no better place than at his own birthday party."

Chapter 8

That night, everyone gathered on the beach to celebrate Frye Fest and Captain Frye's birthday. Party music played over the loudspeakers and everyone was wearing eye patches and pirate hats. A huge barbecue pit had been dug into the sand by the dock. There were hamburgers, hot dogs, lobsters, corn, potatoes, and other delicious treats slowly roasting over the coals.

"Okay, Scooby-Doo," Shaggy said. "It's time for dinner."

"First it's time to catch a ghost," Fred said from behind. "Then we'll have dinner."

Fred walked Shaggy and Scooby away from the crowd and over to the edge of the dock. Daphne, Velma, Uncle Murray, Aunt Maggie, and Salty Joe were waiting there. Next to Salty Joe was an old chest covered with seaweed.

"Here's the plan," Fred said. "Uncle Murray and Aunt Maggie are going to tell everyone that we've found Captain Frye's treasure."

"We have?" Shaggy asked with surprise.

"Not really, Shaggy," Velma said. "It's part of the trap."

"Like, I knew that," Shaggy said. He looked over at the chest and saw two scuba diving outfits next to it.

"Do we have to wear those outfits again?" Shaggy asked.

"Just for show," Daphne said.

"Ruh-uh," Scooby said, shaking his head.

"But there's nothing to be afraid of," Daphne said.

"Roctopus!" Scooby said, waving his paws

around like the eight-armed creature he met in the bay.

"Don't worry, Scooby," Velma said. "We checked out the beach and there's not a single octopus around."

"Look, we don't have much time," Fred said. "Shaggy and Scooby, you put on the scuba outfits. Salty Joe will bring the treasure chest over to the campfire. That should lure Captain Frye out. When he shows up, Uncle Murray and I will catch him with a fishing net."

Aunt Maggie walked over to Scooby-Doo. "Once this is all done, Scooby," she said, "you can have as much as you want to eat."

"Roh roy!" Scooby barked. He grabbed

a scuba mask and put it over his head. He was breathing so heavily he fogged up the glass.

"Daphne, do you remember where you and Fred found the rowing boat earlier?" Velma asked.

"Sure," Daphne said.

"Let's go there," Velma said. "I have a hunch we'll find something interesting." Daphne and Velma walked off down the beach.

"Let's go, everyone," Fred said.

Aunt Maggie and Uncle Murray walked over to the crowd and got everyone's attention. Everyone gasped when Aunt Maggie and Uncle Murray told them about the treasure.

"That's our cue, Scooby-Doo," Shaggy said. He and Scooby walked across the sand to the crowd. Salty Joe followed, carrying the chest on his back. Fred snuck around to the other side of the crowd, holding the fishing net.

Scooby, Shaggy, and Salty Joe entered the middle of the crowd. Salty Joe put the chest down on the sand.

Uncle Murray said to everyone, "These two divers found the treasure in a sunken pirate ship in the bay."

"And they have promised to donate everything they find in the chest to Sandy Cove to help keep our town alive," Aunt Maggie added.

The crowd cheered as Uncle Murray walked over to the chest and knelt down. He used a crowbar to pry open the lid. Everyone in the crowd took a step forward to see what was in the chest. Just then, an explosion came from the water.

Everyone turned and saw Captain Frye walk out of the bay. "Stop!" he bellowed, his voice coming from the loudspeakers. "Give me my treasure or else all of you and this town will be cursed forever!" As the pirate walked towards the crowd, the people moved out of his way. Captain Frye got closer to Shaggy, Scooby, and the treasure chest.

"Now!" Fred called. Fred and Uncle Murray jumped out of the crowd and threw the fishing net over the pirate. Captain Frye gave one quick slash with his sword and the net fell away.

"Must be an old net," Salty Joe said.

"Now you will pay!" Captain Frye yelled.

"Zoinks!" Shaggy cried. "Let's get out of here, Scooby!"

He and Scooby tried to run, but the scuba equipment was too heavy. Scooby took a step in one direction, but the heavy air tanks pulled him in another. Scooby lost his balance and tumbled into Captain Frye. The pirate teetered and then fell into the chest. Scooby was still off balance from the scuba gear. He tried to grab something to keep from falling. His paw hit the lid of the chest and slammed it shut on Captain Frye.

Chapter 9

"**H**elp! Let me out or I'm telling!" Captain
Frye screamed from the chest. Everyone
looked at one another.

"That doesn't sound like a pirate to me,"
Aunt Maggie said.

"Help!" Captain Frye cried.

"Knock it off, you loudmouthed pirate,"
a woman's voice said. It was Edna Crupzak. She
was walking through the crowd, escorted by
Daphne and Velma. She grabbed the crowbar
from Uncle Murray and opened the chest.

"What's this all about?" Salty Joe asked.

"I think I know," Velma said. "First let's see if I'm right."

Salty Joe reached around Captain Frye's neck and gave the pirate's head a turn. Everyone gasped as Salty Joe lifted off the pirate's head. It was a scuba helmet with a pirate mask over it. And inside was Junior Crupzak.

"Junior Crupzak?" Aunt Maggie exclaimed. "I never would have guessed."

"Neither did we at first," Fred said. "The only clue we had was a handful of brochures in a rowing boat."

"A clue that first pointed to Barney Silo," Daphne said.

"But then we put some other things together," Velma added. "Like what Uncle Murray said about the ship being radio-controlled."

"Junior Crupzak was using a radio-controlled dune buggy on the beach," Fred said. "He used his radio-control to take over Uncle Murray's boat and make it sink."

"And I'll bet if you look inside the helmet, you'll find some kind of microphone and transmitter," Velma said. "Junior tuned into the radio station's frequency to get his voice through the speakers and radios."

Aunt Maggie looked at Edna Crupzak. "You've lived here all your life, Edna," Aunt Maggie said. "Why would you ruin the festival and let Barney Silo take over Sandy Cove?"

"Because there really is buried treasure," Velma said. "I confirmed that when I went to the town hall. According to the records, Captain Frye's boat sank with a collection of jewels and other valuables he had stolen."

"And it sank exactly where the ship sank today," Fred explained. "Edna and Junior thought this would help them find the treasure."

Edna nodded her head in agreement. "That's right," she said. "Junior and I were going to use the treasure to buy Shining Palms and knock it down. We wanted to get rid of all the tourists so we could live in peace and quiet. And we would have found the treasure if it wasn't for those meddling kids and their dog."

"Bravo, kids!" Barney Silo said, coming out of the crowd. "You have given me a stroke of inspiration. The legend of Captain Frye is too important. Just look at how many people have come to celebrate him. Let me return Sandy Cove to its former pirate splendour. Everyone  can keep their homes and shops. We'll fix up the place to look like it did when the real Captain Frye lived here."

"Hooray!" the crowd cheered.

BOOM! BOOM! BOOM! Fireworks exploded

in the sky overhead. Coloured lights danced across the sky.

"Well, gang, another mystery solved," Fred said.

"And we owe it all to Scooby-Doo," Aunt Maggie said.

BOOM! BOOM! BOOM! Everyone looked up and saw Scooby-Doo's face in fireworks.

"Scooby-Dooby-Doo!" cheered Scooby.

Solve a Mystery With
Scooby-Doo!

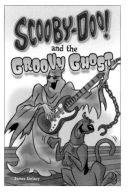

978-1-782-02155-1

978-1-782-02150-6

978-1-782-02152-0

978-1-782-02153-7

SCOOBY-DOO!

← YOU CHOOSE STORIES →

978-1-782-02107-0

978-1-782-02108-7

978-1-782-02109-4

978-1-782-02110-0